The Really Geeky
Sci-Fi Quiz Book

The Really Geeky Sci-Fi Quizbook

© 2012 Mark Ball

Published by Really Geeky
www.geekyquizbooks.com

This edition printed by Lulu
www.lulu.com

Compiled by Mark Ball

All rights reserved. No part of this publication may be reproduced, distributed, or transmitted in any form or by any means, including photocopying, recording, or other electronic or mechanical methods, without the prior written permission of the publisher, except in the case of certain non-commercial uses permitted by copyright law.

ISBN: 978-1-300-44731-3

Table of Contents

Aliens 1
    Multiple Choice 7
    Answers 13
Systems and Worlds 17
    Multiple Choice 21
    Answers 27
Spaceships and Technology 31
    Multiple Choice 36
    Answers 41
Literature 45
    Multiple Choice 50
    Answers 53
TV and Movies 55
    Multiple Choice 62
    Answers 67
Characters and Actors 71
    Multiple Choice 86
    Answers 95
Miscellaneous 103
    Multiple Choice 106
    Answers 109

Aliens

1. By what name is the Yautja species more commonly known?

2. Which TV show featured an alien race called the Taelons?

3. The 90's TV show *Space: Above and Beyond* sees humanity fight a bitter war against which alien species?

4. What is Spock's blood type?

5. What colour is Romulan blood?

6. In the *Star Trek* episode "Arena", Captain Kirk is forced to fight a member of which alien species?

7. In *Star Trek: The Next Generation*, Ensign Ro Larren is a member of what species?

8. In *Star Trek: The Next Generation*, which friendly, law-abiding aliens are native to the planet Rubicun III?

9. In *Star Trek: The Next Generation*, which race of dog-like, humanoid aliens are native to the planet Antica in the Beta Renner System?

10. In *Star Trek: Enterprise*, Doctor Phlox is a member of what species?

11. In *Star Trek: Voyager*, First Maje Jal Cullah is a member of which Delta Quadrant species?

12. In *Star Trek: Voyager*, which alien race pollutes space by thoughtlessly dumping theta radiation?

13. In *Star Trek: Voyager*, Neelix is a member of what species?

14. Of what species is the *Star Trek: Deep Space Nine* character Weyoun?

15. In *Star Trek: Deep Space Nine*, which aliens are addicted to the drug ketracel white?

16. In *Star Trek: Deep Space Nine*, Grand Nagus Zek's mute servant, Maihar'du, was a member of what species?

17. While stationed at Starbase Earheart as a young officer, Jean-Luc Picard was stabbed through the heart by a member of which alien race?

18. Who transported the USS Voyager to the Delta Quadrant?

19. In Ferengi history, who was the first Grand Nagus of the Ferengi Alliance?

20. What is the Borg designation for the Undine species?

21. What is the Borg designation for the human species?

22. In the *Stargate* universe, who built the stargates?

23. Which race of invisible aliens featured in the *Stargate SG-1* episode "Show and Tell"?

24. In *Stargate Atlantis*, Cowen, played by Colm Meaney, was

the leader of which Pegasus Galaxy civilization?

25. In which computer game franchise would you find the Sangheli, Unggoy, and Kig-Yar alien races?

26. Which 1990's sci-fi computer game featured playable alien races such as the Chamachies, the Snovemdomas and the Dubtaks?

27. Which 1990's sci-fi computer game featured playable alien races such as the Klackon, the Mrrshan and the Bulrathi?

28. Which famous alien character is a native of the planet Brodo Asogi?

29. In *Babylon 5*, which alien species became extinct in 2259 following a large-scale outbreak of the Drafa Plague?

30. In *Babylon 5*, what is a Shon'Kar?

31. What was the name of the Vorlon ambassador in *Babylon 5*?

32. What was the name of the Narn ambassador in *Babylon 5*?

33. Which evil aliens originate on the planet Skaro?

34. In what year did the Daleks make their first TV appearance?

35. In *Doctor Who*, what planet is the home-world of the Silurian species?

36. What creature inhabits the Great Pit of Carkoon on the planet Tatooine?

37. The *Star Wars* character Orrimaarko, often referred to as "Prune Face", is a member of what species?

38. In *Star Wars: The Phantom Menace*, Jar Jar Binks is a member of what species?

39. In *Star Wars: The Return of the Jedi*, many members of which species died while delivering information about the second Death Star to the Rebel Alliance?

40. What was the name of the bounty hunter whom Han Solo shot in the Mos Eisley cantina in *Star Wars: A New Hope*?

41. Of what species is the fat blue alien musician Siiruulian Phantele, more commonly known by his stage name, Max Rebo, in the *Star Wars* universe?

42. What is the name of the alien news anchor, or "news monster", in the animated TV show *Futurama*?

43. In *Futurama*, four-armed TV chef Elzar is a member of what species?

44. In the TV series *Farscape*, what species is Zhaan?

45. In the TV series *Farscape*, what species is Ka D'Argo?

46. In the TV series *Farscape*, what species is Aeryn Sun?

47. In the TV series *Farscape*, what species is Rygel?

48. In the TV series *Farscape*, what species is Chiana?

49. Which *Babylon 5* aliens carry their young in a pouch?

50. In the *Doctor Who* episode "Love and Monsters", which British comedian played the hideous Absorbaloff?

51. In the TV show *Andromeda*, what species was the character Rev Bem?

52. In *Battlestar Galactica*, what is the name of the robotic enemies of mankind?

53. In *The Chronicles of Riddick*, Riddick is a member of what species?

54. What was the name of the alien visitor in *The Day the Earth Stood Still*?

55. In the movie *Jurassic Park*, what species of dinosaur spits poison into the eyes of Dennis Nedry?

56. In Larry Niven's *Known Space* series, what alien species are said to be the ancient ancestors of the human race?

57. In L. Ron Hubbard's *Battlefield Earth*, the Earth is ruled by members of which alien species?

58. In H.G Wells' classic novel *The Time Machine*, what was the name of the terrifying subterranean creatures that fed on the Eloi?

59. Which sci-fi show features alien creatures known as Skitters?

60. In the TV show *Falling Skies*, Skitters have how many legs?

61. In *The Hitchhiker's Guide to the Galaxy*, what alien creature assumes that if you can't see it, it can't see you?

62. In the *Doctor Who* episode "Silence in the Library", what was the name of the microscopic lifeforms that had infested

The Library?

63. In which episode of *Star Trek* is Captain Kirk forced to fight a Gorn?

64. Which alien race enjoys the practice of oo-mox?

65. In the *Star Trek: The Next Generation* episode "Samaritan Snare", Lt. LaForge is kidnapped by members of which alien species?

66. In the 2001 movie *Evolution*, what chemical element is used to defeat the aliens?

67. In *Babylon 5*, Droshala is a higher being worshipped by which alien species?

68. Which species of alien, created by Larry Niven, have the appearance of starfish, live on an ice moon, and have the ability to link their nervous systems to form powerful biological supercomputers?

69. The Nistrim, Ogla, Relora and Hobii are sects of which alien race?

70. What species was Denara Pel, the alien scientist with whom The Doctor fell in love in the *Star Trek: Voyager* episode "Lifesigns"?

71. What science fiction TV show features alien races such as the Glish, the Queppu, and the Red Shiny Robots of Vortis?

72. What is Raktajino?

Multiple Choice

73. Which of the following *Stargate* aliens do NOT have the ability to make themselves invisible?
a) The Unas
b) The Reetou
c) The Nox

74. In the *Stargate SG-1* episode "The Fifth Man", a mysterious fifth member of SG-1, Lieutenant Tyler, turns out to be an alien. What is the name of his species?
a) Reetou
b) Reol
c) Gadmeer

75. In the *Alien Nation* science fiction franchise, the alien "Newcomers" are members of which species?
a) Taelon
b) Tenctonese
c) Tzenkethi

76. In the TV show *Babylon 5,* which of the following alien governments is NOT a member of the League of Non-Aligned Worlds?
a) Brakiri Syndicracy
b) Drazi Freehold
c) Narn Regime

77. In *Babylon 5*, what is the Minbari name for the Rangers?
a) Entil'Zha
b) Anla-Shok
c) Do'Shalar

78. In *Babylon 5*, which repulsive, tentacle-faced aliens are described as "carrion eaters"?
a) Hyach

b) Gaim
c) Pak'ma'ra

79. Which of the following alien governments is NOT part of the Babylon 5 Advisory Council?
a) Drazi Freehold
b) Centauri Republic
c) Vorlon Empire

80. Which *Star Wars* aliens are native to the planet Clak'dor VII?
a) Clakonians
b) Bothans
c) Bith

81. In *Star Wars: The Phantom Menace*, the Sith Lord Drarth Maul was a member of which species?
a) Dressellian
b) Dathomirian
c) Diphidian

82. In the expanded *Star Wars* universe, the Sith Lord Darth Plagueis was a member of which species?
a) Phindian
b) Human
c) Muun

83. Born Qymaen jai Sheelal, the rebel leader General Grievous was a member of which alien species?
a) Mustafarian
b) Kaleesh
c) Gorn

84. According to the *Star Trek: Voyager* episode "Distant Origins", the Voth species evolved on which planet?
a) Haakon
b) Tau Ceti IV

c) Earth

85. The Jem'Hadar are the genetically engineered servants of which other alien race?
a) The Romulans
b) The Hirogen
c) The Founders

86. In the Klingon language, what does "Qapla" mean?
a) Honour
b) Success
c) Sorry

87. Mr. Mot, the barber aboard the USS Enterprise in *Star Trek: The Next Generation*, is a member of which alien species?
a) Bolian
b) Tholian
c) Andorian

88. In *Star Trek: Voyager,* Seska is a member of which what alien race?
a) Cardassian
b) Bajoran
c) Kazon

89. In *Star Trek: Enterprise*, Commander Shran is a member of what species?
a) Vulcan
b) Andorian
c) Bolian

90. In *Star Trek: The Next Generation* episode "Manhunt", which fish-like aliens are described by Worf as a "handsome race"?
a) Antedeans
b) Brekkians

c) Hath

91. In *Star Trek: Insurrection*, which aliens stretch their skin in an attempt to appear younger?
a) The Vidiians
b) The Son'a
c) The Xindi

92. In the *Star Trek: The Next Generation* episode "The Outcast", what is unusual about the J'naii species?
a) They are genderless
b) They do not age
c) They have no eyes

93. According to the *Deep Space Nine* episode "Who Mourns for Morn?", where does Morn keep his latinum?
a) In the Bank of Bolius
b) In his mud bath
c) In his second stomach

94. In which *Star Trek: The Next Generation* episode do the Enterprise crew encounter the Borg for the first time?
a) Encounter at Farpoint
b) Deja Q
c) Q Who

95. In Klingon history, what was the name of the tyrant who ruled Qo'noS in the 9th Century before being slain by Kahless the Unforgettable?
a) Duras
b) Molor
c) Klang

96. In Michael Crichton's novel *The Lost World*, which dinosaurs can blend perfectly into the background?
a) Dilophosaurs
b) Velociraptors

c) Carnosaurs

97. Who starred as the alien Sil in the 1995 movie *Species*?
a) Natasha Henstridge
b) Tricia Helfer
c) Milla Jovovich

98. Who starred as the alien Prot in the 2001 movie *K-Pax*?
a) Christian Slater
b) Kevin Spacey
c) Jake Gyllenhaal

99. In Larry Niven's Ringworld, of what species is the character Speaker-to-Animals?
a) Kzinti
b) Tzenkethi
c) Kilrathi

100. The Kilrathi were a species of cat-like warriors in which series of classic computer games?
a) Elite
b) Space Quest
c) Wing Commander

101. In Larry Niven's *Known Space* universe, what happens to Martians when they get wet?
a) They melt
b) They multiply
c) They burst into flames

Answers – Aliens

1. Predators
2. Earth: Final Conflict
3. The Chigs
4. T-negative
5. Green
6. Gorn
7. Bajoran
8. Edo
9. Anticans
10. Denobulan
11. Kazon
12. Malon
13. Talaxian
14. Vorta
15. Jem'Hadar
16. Hupyrian
17. Nausicaan
18. The Caretaker
19. Gint
20. Species 8472
21. Species 5618
22. The Ancients
23. The Reetou
24. The Genii
25. Halo
26. Ascendancy
27. Master of Orion
28. E.T
29. Markab
30. A Narn blood oath
31. Kosh
32. G'kar
33. Daleks
34. 1963

35. Earth
36. Sarlaac
37. Dressellian
38. Gungan
39. Bothans
40. Greedo
41. Ortolan
42. Morbo
43. Neptunian
44. Delvian
45. Luxan
46. Sebacean
47. Hynerian
48. Nebari
49. Narns
50. Peter Kay
51. Magog
52. Cylons
53. Furyan
54. Klaatu
55. Dilophosaurus
56. The Pak
57. Psychlos
58. Morlocks
59. Falling Skies
60. 6
61. The Bugblatter Beast of Traal
62. Vashta Nerada
63. Arena
64. Ferengi
65. Pakleds
66. Selenium
67. Drazi
68. Gw'oth
69. Kazon
70. Vidiian
71. Hyperdrive

72. Klingon coffee
73. a) The Unas
74. b) Reol
75. b) Tenctonese
76. c) Narn Regime
77. b) Anla-Shok
78. c) Pak'ma'ra
79. a) Drazi Freehold
80. c) Bith
81. b) Dathomirian
82. c) Muun
83. b) Kaleesh
84. c) Earth
85. c) The Founders
86. b) Success
87. a) Bolian
88. a) Cardassian
89. b) Andorian
90. a) Antedeans
91. b) The Son'a
92. a) They are genderless
93. c) In his second stomach
94. c) Q Who
95. b) Molor
96. c) Carnosaurs
97. a) Natasha Henstridge
98. b) Kevin Spacey
99. a) Kzinti
100. c) Wing Commander
101. c) They burst into flames

Systems and Worlds

1. What 1956 science fiction movie was set on the planet Altair IV?

2. In *Stargate SG-1*, what planet does Teal'c come from?

3. The sci-fi series *Stargate Atlantis* was set primarily in which galaxy?

4. On what planet was Superman born?

5. Who rules the planet Mongo?

6. What rare substance can only be found on the planet Arakkis?

7. In *The Hitchhiker's Guide to the Galaxy*, Earth is located in which galactic sector?

8. In Isaac Asimov's *Foundation* series, which planet orbits the star Epsilon Eridani and was originally known as Baleyworld?

9. In Isaac Asimov's *Foundation* series, which planet is the home-world of psychohistory developer Hari Seldon?

10. In Isaac Asimov's *Foundation* series, which planet was the capital of the first Galactic Empire?

11. What is the name of the Silver Surfer's home-world?

12. In *Babylon 5*, where was EarthForce One when it was destroyed in 2259, killing President Luis Santiago?

13. The space station Babylon 5 orbits which planet?

14. On which planet was Luke Skywalker raised?

15. What planet do Wookies come from?

16. On which world do the Ewoks live?

17. On which planet does Luke Skywalker meet Jedi Master Yoda?

18. In *Star Wars: The Phantom Menace*, which planet is the home-world of the Gungans?

19. In the *Star Wars* prequel films, the Republic's clone army was bred on which world?

20. In *Star Wars: The Empire Strikes Back*, Cloud City is located above which planet?

21. The space-port of Mos Eisley is located on which planet in the *Star Wars* universe?

22. In *Star Wars*, which town is famously described by Obi-Wan Kenobi as a "wretched hive of scum and villainy"?

23. On which planet in the *Star Wars* universe would you find the town of Mos Espa?

24. In which *Star Wars* movie do Obi-Wan Kenobi, Qui-Gon Jinn and Padme Amidala visit the town of Mos Espa?

25. Quo'nos is the home-world of which alien race?

26. In *Star Trek: The Next Generation,* the android Data was built on which world?

27. In *Star Trek: Enterprise*, on which planet do the Aenar originate?

28. The Bajoran Wormhole links the Alpha Quadrant with which other galactic quadrant?

29. In the *Star Trek: The Next Generation* episode, "The Price", two Ferengi are stranded in the Delta Quadrant while studying which wormhole?

30. On the planet Risa, what would you display if you were interested in "jamaharon"?

31. In the TV show *Doctor Who*, what was the name of the Time Lord's home planet?

32. In *Doctor Who*, which aliens come from the planet Raxacoricofallapatorian?

33. Skaro is the home-world of which evil aliens?

34. On which TV show would you see the worlds Ariel, Greenleaf, Bernadette, and Whitefall?

35. In the TV series *Firefly*, Simon and River Tam grew up on which planet?

36. On which planet in the *Firefly* universe would you find the Eavesdown Docks?

37. In the TV show *Andromeda*, what planet was the home-world of the Than-Thre-Kull?

38. In the TV show *Andromeda*, what planet was the homeworld of the amphibious Bamiya species?

39. In *Battlestar Galactica*, mankind is said to have lived alongside the gods on which planet?

40. In *Battlestar Galactica*, which planet is described as the "food basket" of the Twelve Colonies?

41. In *Battlestar Galactica*, the "Temple of Five" is located on which planet?

42. In the TV series *Caprica*, the Ha'la'tha crime organisation originates on which of the twelve worlds?

43. Gerry Anderson's science fiction series *Space 1999* was set where?

44. The mid-90's TV series *Earth 2* was set on which planet?

45. In the TV comedy *Mork and Mindy*, Mork was a visitor from which planet?

46. The 1984 film *Dune* is set primarily on what planet?

47. On what planet is the movie *Alien 3* set?

48. In the 1986 movie *Flight of the Navigator*, what planet is Max is trying to return to?

49. In the movie *K-Pax*, the alien Prot comes from what planet?

50. In the classic science fiction movie *This Island Earth*, what was the name of Exeter's home planet?

51. The 1963 Philip K. Dick novel *The Game Players of Titan*

is set on which planet?

52. In Frank Herbert's science fiction novel *Dune,* which planet is the ancestral home of the House Atreides?

53. Isaac Asimov's science fiction novel *The Naked Sun* sees detective Elijah Bailey and robot R. Daneel Olivaw visit which world to solve an unusual murder mystery?

54. In *Starship Troopers*, the "Bugs" (also referred to as "Arachnids") originate on which world?

55. In *Futurama*, who is the ruler of the planet Omicron Persei 8?

56. In *The Restaurant at the End of the Universe*, prehistoric Earth is colonized by hairdressers and telephone sanitisers from what planet?

57. What was the name of the library planet visited by the USS Enterprise in the *Star Trek* episode "The Lights of Zatar"?

58. In *Star Trek: Voyager*, Species 8472 come from what region of space?

59. In the animated show *Invader Zim*, what planet is Zim from?

60. In the novel *Slaughterhouse-Five*, Billy Pilgrim is transported to which alien world?

Multiple Choice

61. In *Stargate Atlantis*, Ronon Dex is a native of which world?

a) Athos
b) Phaelon
c) Sateda

62. In *Stargate Atlantis*, Teyla Emmagen is a native of which world?
a) Athos
b) Sateda
c) Abydos

63. In *Stargate SG-1*, Jonas Quinn's home-world, Langara, is rich in which rare element?
a) Naqahdah
b) Naqahdriah
c) Trinium

64. Which *Stargate* planet is thought to be the evolutionary home of both the Goa'uld and the Unas?
a) P3X-888
b) P2A-347
c) PX7-941

65. After the defeat of the Goa'uld, which planet is named as the capital of the Free Jaffa Nation in *Stargate SG-1*?
a) Chulak
b) Dakara
c) Kheb

66. In the TV series *Babylon 5*, where is the government of the Earth Alliance based?
a) Geneva, Switzerland
b) Buenos Ares, Argentina
c) Kyoto, Japan

67. Supreme Commander of the Droid Army, General Grievous, was killed fighting Obi-Wan Kenobi on which planet?

a) Mustafar
b) Utapau
c) Geonosis

68. On which planet was Han Solo born?
a) Corellia
b) Yavin
c) Malastare

69. Princess Leia Organa was raised on which world?
a) Coruscant
b) Alderaan
c) Naboo

70. In the *Star Wars* universe, the Aqualish species are native to which planet?
a) Ando
b) Kamino
c) Dac

71. The pig-like Ugnuaghts are native to which planet in the *Star Wars* universe?
a) Dantooine
b) Malastare
c) Gentes

72. In *Star Trek*, Janus 6 is the home-world of which alien species?
a) Janusians
b) Volians
c) Horta

73. In the original series *Star Trek* episode "Space Seed", Captain Kirk maroons Khan on which planet?
a) Ceti Alpha 5
b) Ceti Alpha 6
c) Tau Alpha C

74. In *Star Trek VI: The Undiscovered Country*, Captain Kirk is sentenced to life imprisonment on which world?
a) Praxis
b) Rura Penthe
c) Remus

75. The movie *Star Trek: Nemesis* sees the crew of the Enterprise visit which twin worlds?
a) Caprica and Gemenon
b) Ceti Alpha 5 and Ceti Alpha 6
c) Romulus and Remus

76. USS Voyager's Talaxian crew member, Neelix, was born on which world?
a) Ocampa
b) Talax
c) Rinax

77. In *Star Trek: Deep Space Nine*, the Denorios Belt is located at the edge of which star system?
a) The Amargosa system
b) The Bajoran system
c) The Chin'toka system

78. In *Star Trek: Enterprise*, the Xindi originate in which region of space?
a) Fluidic space
b) Denorios Belt
c) Delphic Expanse

79. In the animated show *Futurama*, what new name was given to the planet Uranus in the year 2620?
a) Urectum
b) Urgina
c) Urmomma

80. In the animated series *Futurama*, where is Robot Hell located?
a) Mercury
b) The Galaxy of Terror
c) New Jersey

81. In *Futurama* who lives at the north pole of the planet Neptune?
a) Santa
b) The Yeti
c) The Penguin King

82. The 1995 movie *Screamers* was set on which planet?
a) Sirius 6B
b) Fury 161
c) LV-223

83. In the DC universe, the Guardians of the Universe evolved on which world?
a) Maltus
b) Krypton
c) Klendathu

84. In Larry Niven's *Known Space* series, which planet is the home-world of the Grogs?
a) Whig
b) Jinx
c) Down

85. In Larry Niven's *Known Space* series, the planet Wunderland orbits which star?
a) Alpha Centauri
b) Vega
c) Betelgeuse

86. On which planet are you most likely to find a horga'hn?
a) Janus 6

b) Risa
c) Quo'nos

87. Which word does the *Hitchhiker's Guide to the Galaxy* use to describe the Earth?
a) Harmless
b) Pointless
c) Overrated

Answers – Systems and Worlds

1. Forbidden Planet
2. Chulak
3. Pegasus Galaxy
4. Krypton
5. Ming the Merciless
6. The spice Melange
7. ZZ9 Plural Z Alpha
8. Comporellon
9. Helicon
10. Trantor
11. Zen-La
12. The transfer point off Io
13. Epsilon 3
14. Tatooine
15. Kashyyyk
16. The forest moon of Endor
17. Dagobah
18. Naboo
19. Kamino
20. Bespin
21. Tatooine
22. Mos Eisley
23. Tatooine
24. Star Wars: The Phantom Menace
25. Klingons
26. Omicron Theta
27. Andoria
28. Gamma Quadrant
29. The Barzan Wormhole
30. A horga'hn
31. Gallifrey
32. Slitheen
33. Daleks
34. Firefly

35. Osiris
36. Persephone
37. San-Ska-Re
38. Infinity Atoll
39. Kobol
40. Aerilon
41. The Algae Planet
42. Tauron
43. Moonbase Alpha
44. G889
45. Ork
46. Arrakis
47. Fury 161
48. Phaelon
49. K-Pax
50. Metaluna
51. Earth
52. Caladan
53. Solaria
54. Klendathu
55. Lrrr
56. Golgafrincham
57. Memory Alpha
58. Fluidic space
59. Irk
60. Tralfamadore
61. c) Sateda
62. a) Athos
63. b) Naqahdriah
64. a) P3X-888
65. b) Dakara
66. a) Geneva, Switzerland
67. b) Utapau
68. a) Corellia
69. b) Alderaan
70. a) Ando
71. c) Gentes

72. c) Horta
73. a) Ceti Alpha 5
74. b) Rura Penthe
75. c) Romulus and Remus
76. c) Rinax
77. b) The Bajoran system
78. c) Delphic Expanse
79. a) Urectum
80. c) New Jersey
81. a) Santa
82. a) Sirius 6B
83. a) Maltus
84. c) Down
85. a) Alpha Centauri
86. b) Risa
87. a) Harmless

Spaceships and Technology

1. According to *Star Trek: The Next Generation*, what is the correct matter/antimatter ratio needed to create a stable warp field?

2. How many stargate symbols are required to 'dial' a planet within the Milky Way galaxy?

3. Under normal circumstances, what is the maximum time that a stargate can remain open?

4. The TV series *Firefly* centred on the crew of which spaceship?

5. In *Star Trek: Deep Space Nine*, which Federation starship is fitted with a Romulan cloaking device?

6. In the original series of *Star Trek*, what is the registry number of the USS Enterprise?

7. In *Star Trek: Deep Space Nine*, what is the registry number of the USS Defiant?

8. In the *Star Trek: Voyager* episode "Relativity", who was captain of the Federation time-ship USS Relativity?

9. In *Star Trek: Voyager*, Rudolph Ransom was captain of which Federation starship?

10. Aboard which Federation Starship did Tuvok first serve as an Ensign?

12. In the movie *Star Trek II: The Wrath of Khan*, which ship does Khan take into battle against the Enterprise?

12. In the *Star Trek* episode "Space Seed", Khan Noonien Singh is found drifting through space aboard which spaceship?

13. In the movie *Star Trek: First Contact*, what is the name of Zefram Cochrane's experimental warp ship?

14. In the *Star Trek: The Next Generation* episode "Cause and Effect", the Enterprise encounters which Soyuz-class starship after it has been lost in a temporal anomaly for 90 years?

15. After his service aboard the USS Enterprise, Hikaru Sulu went on to serve as Captain of which Federation starship?

16. In the *Star Trek: The Next Generation* episode "The Wounded", the Enterprise travels into Cardassian space to intercept which renegade Federation starship?

17. The classic computer game Wing Commander and its 1999 movie adaptation were set aboard which spaceship?

18. Under which mountain is Stargate Command located?

19. In *Stargate SG-1* and *Stargate Atlantis*, which ship is commanded by Colonel Steven Caldwell?

20. What space station is 5 miles long, rotates to create gravity, and is described as the "last, best hope for peace"?

21. The *Babylon 5* spin-off series *Crusade* follows the adventures of which Interstellar Alliance spaceship?

22. In the *Star Trek: The Next Generation* episode "Times Arrow", what futuristic artifact is found at an archaeological dig site in San Francisco?

23. What was the original Cardassian name for space station Deep Space Nine?

24. In the *Star Trek* episode "The Trouble With Tribbles", the Enterprise becomes infested with tribbles while visiting which space station?

25. In the animated show *Futurama*, Captain Zapp Brannigan commands which battleship?

26. In *Battlestar Galactica*, which was the only battlestar besides the Galactica to escape the Cylon attack on the colonies?

27. What was the name of the prison ship in the TV show *Battlestar Galactica*?

28. According to the TV series *Caprica,* what is the term "Cylon" short for?

29. Which TV show was set aboard the Satellite of Love?

30. In the *Star Trek: The Next Generation* episode "Captain's Holiday", Captain Picard teams up with Vash to find which ancient alien artefact?

31. The TV series *Space: Above and Beyond* followed a group of US marines stationed aboard which spaceship?

32. What was the name of the intelligent robot in the 1986 family movie *Short Circuit*?

33. What is the name of the robot in *The Day the Earth Stood Still*?

34. In the movie *Blade Runner*, how long are the Nexus-6 replicants supposed live?

35. What was the name of the luxury passenger liner in the animated film *Wall-E*?

36. What spaceship is featured in the 1999 movie *Galaxy Quest*?

37. What was the name of the alien communication device seen in the classic science fiction movie *This Island Earth*?

38. The 1979 blockbuster *Alien* was set aboard which ship?

39. In the movie *Aliens*, Ripley accompanies a unit of marines to the planet LV-426 aboard which spaceship?

40. Which 2007 science fiction movie was set aboard the spaceship Icarus 2?

41. In the movie *Men in Black*, what device to the agents use to wipe people's memories?

42. Marineville was the home of which high-tech submarine?

43. In the TV series *Farscape*, the living spaceship Moya gives birth to another spaceship. What was it's name?

44. In *Star Trek: Voyager*, what does the acronym E.M.H stand for?

45. In H.G Wells' *The War of the Worlds*, which British Navy ship destroys a Martian war machine?

46. In the *Back to the Future* films, how fast must the DeLorean reach in order to travel through time?

47. What was the name of the Robinson family's spaceship in *Lost in Space*?

48. In the TV show *Lost*, what piece of technology prevents the Smoke Monster from entering the village?

49. Which spaceship was commanded by Colonel Steve Zodiac of the World Space Patrol?

50. Which science fiction series featured computers called Zen, Orac, and Slave?

51. What spaceship provided the setting for the sci-fi comedy series *Hyperdrive*?

52. In *Star Trek IV: The Voyage Home*, what name did Kirk and his crew give to their captured Klingon Bird of Prey?

53. In *Doctor Who*, what does the acronym TARDIS stand for?

54. What type of vehicle was Thunderbird 4?

55. What movie featured a flying robot named Weebo?

56. What movie featured a robot named Dot Matrix?

57. In the TV series Lost, what does the acronym DHARMA stand for?

58. According to the classic science fiction movie *This Island Earth*, a "bead condenser", an "intensifier disk", and a "cathermin tube with an inindium complex of +4" are some of the 2486 components needed to make a what?

Multiple Choice

59. In *Stargate SG-1*, what name was given to the first American-built spaceship to be capable of interstellar travel?
a) Daedalus
b) Prometheus
c) Phoenix

60. The sci-fi spin-off series *Stargate Universe* was set aboard which spaceship?
a) Destiny
b) Serenity
c) Aurora

61. In *Star Trek: The Next Generation*, the D'deridex-class is a type of spaceship used by which enemy of the Federation?
a) The Cardassian Union
b) The Klingon Empire
c) The Romulan Empire

62. In *Star Trek: The Next Generation*, which Alpha Quadrant species uses Galor-class and Keldon-class starships?
a) Klingons
b) Cardassians
c) Ferengi

63. K'Tinga, Negh'Var and Vor'Cha are types of starship used by which species?
a) Klingons
b) Jem'Hadar
c) Breen

64. Which starship was Captain Jean-Luc Picard's first command?

a) USS Potemkin
b) USS Stargazer
c) USS Hood

65. At the end of the movie *Star Trek: Nemesis*, Will Riker leaves the Enterprise to take command of which vessel?
a) USS Ares
b) USS Tripoli
c) USS Titan

66. The android Data was found on the planet Omicron Theta and reactivated by the crew of which starship?
a) USS Lexington
b) USS Tripoli
c) USS Havana

67. In the *Star Trek: The Next Generation* movies, what class of starship is the USS Enterprise-E?
a) Sovereign-class
b) Galaxy-class
c) Ambassador-class

68. In *Star Trek: The Next Generation*, what class of starship was the USS Enterprise-C?
a) Miranda-class
b) Galaxy-class
c) Ambassador-class

69. In the *Star Trek: Voyager* episode "Message in a Bottle", The Doctor is transported across the galaxy to which federation starship?
a) USS Equinox
b) USS Dauntless
c) USS Prometheus

70. What is the registry number of the USS Voyager?
a) NCC-74656

b) NCC-74205
c) NCC-72408

71. What class of starship is the USS Voyager?
a) Nova-class
b) Intrepid-class
c) Miranda-class

72. What is the registry number of the Intrepid-class USS Bellerophon, a Federation starship under the command of Admiral Ross during the Dominion War?
a) NCC-62048
b) NCC-63549
c) NCC-74705

73. When the USS Defiant was destroyed during the Second Battle of the Chin'toka System, which starship was renamed Defiant and assigned to Captain Sisko as a replacement?
a) USS Sao Paulo
b) USS Valiant
c) USS Bellerophon

74. In the movie *Star Trek: Nemesis* what is the name of Praetor Shinzon's heavily armed battleship?
a) Negh'Var
b) Valdore
c) Scimitar

75. During the Dominion War, Worf's son, Alexander Rozhenko, served aboard which ship?
a) USS Thunderchild
b) IRW Devoras
c) IKS Rotarran

76. Which Oberth-class Federation Starship was destroyed by Wesley Crusher in the *TNG* episode "The Naked Now"?
a) USS Grissom

b) USS Hawking
c) SS Tsiolkovsky

77. In the pilot episode of *Star Trek: Deep Space Nine*, titled "Emissary", Commander Sisko serves aboard which starship during the battle of Wolf 359?
a) USS Bozeman
b) USS Saratoga
c) USS Potemkin

78. In the movie *Star Trek: Generations*, the Enterprise crew rescue the Elorian bartender Guinan from which crippled transport ship?
a) Lakul
b) Kobayashi Maru
c) Hitei Kan

79. In the *Futurama* episode "I Dated a Robot", Fry buys a robotic imitation of actress Lucy Liu from which website?
a) Kidnappster
b) eBot
c) The Pirate eBay

80. In the *Battlestar Galactica* episode "Flesh and Bone", a Cylon is discovered hiding aboard which ship?
a) Olympic Carrier
b) Gemenon Traveller
c) Virgon Express

81. The movie *Alien Resurrection* is set aboard which spaceship?
a) USM Auriga
b) TCS Midway
c) ESCS Olympus

82. In *Buck Rodgers in the 25th Century*, what was Dr. Theopolis?

a) A robot
b) A computer
c) A brain in a jar

83. Before being assigned to Babylon 5, Captain John Sheridan commanded which ship?
a) EAS Achilles
b) EAS Prometheus
c) EAS Agamemnon

84. Lieutenant Commander Data has what type of brain?
a) Positronic
b) Duotronic
c) Cybernetic

85. How did Han Solo acquire the Millennium Falcon?
a) He stole it
b) He won it in a bet
c) It was a gift

Answers – Spaceships and Technology

1. A ratio of 1:1
2. 7
3. 38 minutes
4. Serenity
5. USS Defiant
6. NCC-1701
7. NX-74205
8. Captain Braxton
9. USS Equinox
10. USS Excelsior
11. USS Reliant
12. SS Botany Bay
13. Phoenix
14. USS Bozeman
15. USS Excelsior
16. USS Phoenix
17. The Tiger's Claw
18. Cheyenne Mountain
19. USS Daedalus
20. Babylon 5
21. Excalibur
22. Data's head
23. Terok Nor
24. Deep Space K-7
25. The Nimbus
26. Battlestar Pegasus
27. Astral Queen
28. Cybernetic Life-form Node
29. Mystery Science Theatre 3000
30. The Tox Uthat
31. USS Saratoga
32. Johnny 5
33. Gort
34. 4 years

35. Axium
36. NSEA Protector
37. The "Interocitor"
38. Nostromo
39. Sulaco
40. Sunshine
41. Neuralizer
42. Stingray
43. Talyn
44. Emergency Medical Hologram
45. HMS Thunderchild
46. 88 mph
47. Jupiter 2
48. The sonar fence
49. Fireball XL5
50. Blake's 7
51. HMS Camden Lock
52. HMS Bounty
53. Time and Relative Dimension in Space
54. Submarine
55. Flubber
56. Space Balls
57. Department of Heuristics and Research on Material Applications
58. An "Interocitor"
59. b) Prometheus
60. a) Destiny
61. c) The Romulan Empire
62. b) Cardassians
63. a) Klingons
64. b) USS Stargazer
65. c) USS Titan
66. b) USS Tripoli
67. a) Sovereign-class
68. c) Ambassador-class
69. c) USS Prometheus
70. a) NCC-74656

71. b) Intrepid-class
72. c) NCC-74705
73. a) USS Sao Paulo
74. c) Scimitar
75. c) IKS Rotarran
76. c) SS Tsiolkovsky
77. b) USS Saratoga
78. a) Lakul
79. a) Kidnappster
80. b) Gemenon Traveller
81. a) USM Auriga
82. b) A computer
83. c) EAS Agamemnon
84. a) Positronic
85. b) He won it in a bet

Literature

1. In what year was the classic science fiction novel *The War of the Worlds* first published?

2. In the work of Karel Čapek, what does *R.U.R* stand for?

3. The 1951 film *The Thing From Another World* was based on which novella by John W. Campbell Jr.?

4. Originally published in 1960, which novel by Philip K. Dick depicts a world where humanity is ruled by a super-computer known as Vulcan 3?

5. In which 1966 science fiction novel does organ-transplant doctor Eric Sweetscent get caught up in a war between two alien species, the Starmen and the Reegs?

6. Which 1957 science fiction novel sees detective Elijah Bailey and robot R. Daneel Olivaw visit the world of Solaria to solve an unusual murder mystery?

7. Kevin Costner starred in the 1997 film adaptation of which novel by David Brin?

8. Who wrote the science fiction novel *The Planet of the Apes*?

9. Who wrote the science fiction novel *Dhalgren*?

10. The Humanx Commonwealth is an interstellar political entity that features in the works of which science fiction author?

11. Who wrote the 1966 science fiction novel *Flowers for Algernon*?

12. Who wrote the science fiction novel *The Moon is a Harsh Mistress*, which tells the story of a lunar colony's revolt against Earth-rule?

13. Who wrote the 1985 novel *The Cat Who Walks Through Walls*?

14. Tralfamadore is the name of a fictional planet used frequently by which science fiction author?

15. Which science fiction author wrote the classic novel *The First Men in the Moon*?

16. Which science fiction author wrote the novel *The War in the Air*?

17. Which science fiction author wrote the novel *In the Days of the Comet*?

18. Which science fiction author wrote *From the Earth to the Moon*?

19. Which famous science fiction author wrote *Eight Hundred Leagues on the Amazon*?

20. Which famous science fiction author wrote the novel *Martian Time-Slip*?

21. Who wrote the dystopian novel *Brave New World*?

22. Who wrote the cyberpunk novel *Neuromancer*?

23. Who wrote the novels *The Caves of Steel*, *The Naked Sun* and *The Robots of Dawn*?

24. Which author wrote *The Day of The Triffids*, *The Chrysalids* and *The Midwich Cuckoos*?

25. Who wrote *The Trouble With Lichen*?

26. Who wrote the 1982 novel *Battlefield Earth*?

27. Who wrote the 1970 Hugo Award winning novel *Ringworld*?

28. *The Goddess of Ganymede* was the first published novel of which science fiction writer?

29. Who wrote the 1974 novel *The Forever War*?

30. Who wrote the 1978 multi award winning novel *Gateway*?

31. Who wrote the novel *The Andromeda Strain*?

32. Who wrote the 1985 Nebula Award and 1986 Hugo Award winning novel *Ender's Game*?

33. Who wrote the novel *The Coming of the Quantum Cats*?

34. Who wrote the 1976 Nebula Award winning novel *Man Plus*?

35. Who wrote the 1989 novel *TekWar*, with uncredited help from author Ron Goulart?

36. Published in 1950, *The Martian Chronicles* is a short story collection by which celebrated science fiction writer?

37. *Solar Lottery* was the first published novel of which prolific science fiction author?

38. *Our Friends from Frolix 8* is a novel by which prolific science fiction writer?

39. Who wrote the 1964 novel *The Simulacra*?

40. Who wrote the Hugo Award and Nebula Award winning novella *Beggars in Spain*?

41. Who wrote the 2003 Nebula award winning novel *The Speed of Dark*?

42. Who wrote the Hugo and Nebula award winning novel *American Gods*?

43. Who wrote the 1959 novel *The Sirens of Titan*?

44. Which science fiction novel refers to its protagonist simply as "The Time Traveller"?

45. What is the name of the protagonist in H.G Wells' *The Island of Dr. Moreau*?

46. What is the name of the protagonist in John Wyndham's *The Day of the Triffids*?

47. Rick Deckard is the protagonist in which science fiction novel?

48. Horselover Fat is the protagonist of which novel by Philip K. Dick?

49. In what 1980 science fiction novel by Gregory Bentford do scientists send a message through time, warning the past of

an impending environmental catastrophe?

50. The 1995 movie *Johnny Mnemonic* was adapted from a short story by which science fiction writer?

51. The classic science fiction horror movie *The Village of the Damned* was based on which novel by John Wyndham?

52. Who wrote the novel on which the 1993 movie *Jurassic Park* was based?

53. The movies *Minority Report*, *Total* Recall, *Next* and *The Adjustment Bureau* were based on the work of which science fiction writer?

54. Who wrote the famous "three laws of robotics"?

55. Who wrote the comic book series *V for Vendetta*, *Watchmen*, and *From Hell*?

56. Who write the dystopian novel *A Clockwork Orange*?

57. Which 1969 novel tells the story of Billy Pilgrim, a World War II veteran who has become unstuck in time?

58. What science fiction novel opens with the line "When a day that you happen to know is Wednesday starts of by sounding like a Sunday, there is something seriously wrong somewhere"?

59. What science fiction novel opens with the line "Once upon a time there was a Martian called Valentine Michael Smith"?

60. Who wrote the 1961 novel *Stranger in a Strange Land*?

Multiple Choice

61. According to the *Hitchhiker's Guide to the Galaxy*, who wrote the books "Where God Went Wrong", "Some More of God's Greatest Mistakes", and "Who is this God Person Anyway"?
a) Slartibartfast
b) Zaphod Beeblebrox
c) Oolon Colluphid

62. Who is credited as being the first person to use the word "robot"?
a) Josef Čapek
b) Isaac Asimov
c) H.G Wells

63. In H.G Wells' *The Time Machine*, the time traveller meets the Eloi and Morlocks in which future year?
a) 2803 AD
b) 8503 AD
c) 802,701 AD

64. Which 1970's science fiction movie was based on the novel *Make Room! Make Room!* by Harry Harrison?
a) Soylent Green
b) Logan's Run
c) The Terminal Man

65. The 2001 movie *AI: Artificial Intelligence* is based on the work of which prolific science fiction writer?
a) Brian Aldiss
b) Ray Bradbury
c) Arthur C. Clarke

66. Who wrote the comedic science fiction novel *Starship Titanic*?

a) Rob Grant
b) Douglas Adams
c) Terry Jones

67. Who wrote the 1992 Hugo Award winning novel *A Fire Upon the Deep*?
a) Orson Scott Card
b) Vernor Vinge
c) Elizabeth Moon

68. Valentine Michael Smith, is the Martian-raised protagonist of which Robert A. Heinlein novel?
a) Stranger in a Strange Land
b) Between Planets
c) Methuselah's Children

69. Which character takes the central role in Isaac Asimov's *The Naked Sun*?
a) Droyden Moon
b) Elijah Baley
c) Edward Prentice

70. In what year was the classic science fiction novel *The Time Machine* first published?
a) 1885
b) 1895
c) 1905

71. In what year was Jules Verne's adventure novel *A Journey to the Centre of the Earth* first published?
a) 1864
b) 1874
c) 1884

Answers – Literature

1. 1898
2. Rossum's Universal Robots
3. Who Goes There?
4. Vulcan's Hammer
5. Now Wait for Last Year
6. The Naked Sun
7. The Postman
8. Pierre Boulle
9. Samuel R. Delany
10. Alan Dean Foster
11. Daniel Keyes
12. Robert A. Heinlein
13. Robert A. Heinlein
14. Kurt Vonnegut
15. H.G Wells
16. H.G Wells
17. H.G Wells
18. Jules Verne
19. Jules Verne
20. Philip K. Dick
21. Aldous Huxley
22. William Gibson
23. Isaac Asimov
24. John Wyndham
25. John Wyndham
26. L. Ron Hubbard
27. Larry Niven
28. Mike Resnick
29. Joe Haldeman
30. Frederik Pohl
31. Michael Crichton
32. Orson Scott Card
33. Frederick Pohl
34. Frederick Pohl

35. William Shatner
36. Ray Bradbury
37. Philip K. Dick
38. Philip K. Dick
39. Philip K. Dick
40. Nancy Kress
41. Elizabeth Moon
42. Neil Gaiman
43. Kurt Vonnegut
44. The Time Machine
45. Edward Prentice
46. Bill Masen
47. Do Androids Dream of Electric Sheep?
48. VALIS
49. Timescape
50. William Gibson
51. The Midwich Cuckoos
52. Michael Crichton
53. Philip K. Dick
54. Isaac Asimov
55. Alan Moore
56. Anthony Burgess
57. Slaughterhouse-Five
58. The Day of the Triffids
59. Stranger in a Strange Land
60. Robert A. Heinlein
61. c) Oolon Colluphid
62. a) Josef Čapek
63. c) 802,701 AD
64. a) Soylent Green
65. a) Brian Aldiss
66. c) Terry Jones
67. b) Vernor Vinge
68. a) Stranger in a Strange Land
69. b) Elijah Baley
70. b) 1895
71. a) 1864

TV and Movies

1. In the movie *Back to the Future*, Marty McFly time-travels to what year?

2. Which science fiction movie used the promotional tag-line "Man is the warmest place to hide"?

3. Which science fiction movie used the promotional tag-line "The thing that won't die, in the nightmare that won't end"?

4. Which science fiction movie used the promotional tag-line "Everybody runs"?

5. Which science fiction movie used the promotional tag-line "Whoever wins... We lose"?

6. Which science fiction movie used the promotional tag-line "The future begins"?

7. Which science fiction movie used the promotional tag-line "Nice planet, we'll take it!"?

8. Which science fiction movie used the promotional tag-line "Justice needs a new program"?

9. Which 1986 movie used the tag-line "There can be only one"?

10. In what year were the science fiction films *Waterworld*,

Species, *Judge Dredd* and *Johnny Mnemonic* all released?

11. In what year were the science fiction films *Galaxy Quest*, *The Matrix*, *Bicentennial Man* and the movie adaptation of the computer game *Wing Commander* all released?

12. In what year was Ridley Scott's science fiction horror movie *Alien* released?

13. In what year were the films *Blade Runner*, *E.T. The Extra-Terrestrial* and *Tron* all released?

14. In what year was the Oscar-winning blockbuster *Avatar* released?

15. In what year was the film *Star Trek: Generations* released?

16. In what year was the film *Star Trek II: The Wrath of Khan* released?

17. In what year was John Carpenter's science fiction horror *The Thing* released?

18. What year was the science fiction blockbuster *Independence Day* released?

19. What year saw the release of the classic science fiction movie *Forbidden Planet*?

20. What year saw the release of the classic science fiction movies *The Man from Planet X*, *The Thing from Another World*, and *The Day the Earth Stood Still*?

21. What year saw the release of the classic science fiction movies *Earth vs. the Spider*, *Frankenstein 1970*, and *Attack of the 50 Foot Woman*?

22. What year saw the release of the classic science fiction movies *Silent Running*, *The Thing with Two Heads*, and *Beware! The Blob*?

23. Who directed the science fiction films *28 Days Later* and *Sunshine*?

24. Who directed the 1979 film *Alien*?

25. Who directed the 1984 movie adaptation of Frank Herbert's *Dune*?

26. Who directed the 2001 remake of *Planet of the Apes*, but said he'd "rather jump out a window" than make a sequel?

27. Who directed the 1996 comedy *Mars Attacks!*?

28. Who directed the 1998 movie *Armageddon*?

29. Who directed the 1982 movie *Blade Runner*?

30. Who directed the movies *Stargate*, *Independence Day* and *The Day after Tomorrow*?

31. Who directed the 2002 movie *Minority Report*?

32. Who directed the 1960 film adaptation of H.G Wells' *The Time Machine*?

33. Who directed the 2002 film adaptation of H.G Wells' classic novel *The Time Machine*?

34. Who directed the 2005 remake of *The War of the Worlds*?

35. Who directed the 2009 movie adaptation of *Star Trek*?

36. Who directed the 2009 science fiction blockbuster *Avatar*?

37. Who directed the 1927 cult-classic *Metropolis*?

38. Who directed *Star Trek III: The Search for Spock*?

39. Who directed *Star Trek IV: The Voyage Home*?

40. Who directed *Star Trek V: The Final Frontier*?

41. Who directed *Star Trek VI: The Undiscovered Country*?

42. Who directed *Star Trek: First Contact*?

43. Who directed the 2004 disaster movie *The Day After Tomorrow*?

44. Who directed the 2007 film *Transformers*?

45. In which science fiction TV show would you find the characters Hoban Washburne, Jayne Cobb and Inarra Serra?

46. In which sci-fi show would you find the characters Dylan Hunt, Beka Valentine and Trance Gemini?

47. Lorne Greene, Terry Carter, Richard Hatch, and Dirk Benedict made up the primary cast of which 1970's sci-fi show?

48. In which sci-fi show would you find the characters D'Argo, Chiana and Zhaan?

49. Quinn Mallory, Wade Welles, Rembrandt Brown and Professor Arturo were characters in which 90's sci-fi show?

50. In which sci-fi show would you find the characters Wilma Deering, Twiki and Dr Theopolis?

51. In which sci-fi show would you find the characters Echo, Victor and Topher Brink?

52. In which TV show would you find the characters Colonel White, Destiny Angel and Lieutenant Green?

53. Which famous actor appeared as the Big Giant Head in the TV comedy *Third Rock from the Sun*?

54. What 1986 movie featured a Trimaxian Drone Ship from the planet Phaelon, a Puckmaren, and robot named RALF?

55. In which film does the "Rage Virus" wipe out the population of Great Britain?

56. In what movie does Tom Cruise star as John Anderton, a detective in the pre-crime department of Washington D.C's police force?

57. In which Star Wars movie does Darth Vader reveal to Luke that he is the boy's father?

58. What is "Soylent Green" made from?

59. The short-lived science fiction series *Crusade* was a spin-off of which earlier TV show?

60. In what year did the science fiction series *Babylon 5* first air?

61. In what year did *Star Trek: The Next Generation* first air?

62. In what year did *Star Trek: Deep Space Nine* first air?

63. In what year did *Star Trek: Voyager* first air?

64. In what year did the original *Star Trek* series first air?

65. In which episode did the omnipotent prankster "Q" make his only *Star Trek: Deep Space Nine* appearance?

66. In which *Star Trek* episode did Joan Collins play social worker Edith Keeler?

67. In what year did *The X Files* first air?

68. Mel Smith and Griff Rhys Jones starred in which 1985 science fiction comedy?

69. Which two screenwriters and producers are credited with creating the TV show *Stargate SG-1*?

70. In what year was the futuristic cartoon *The Jetsons* first aired?

71. Which science fiction movie sees Will Smith punch an alien in the face and say "Welcome to Earth"?

72. Which actor played the role of President of the United States in the 1998 movie *Deep Impact*?

73. Casper Van Dien starred as Johnny Rico in which 1997 sci-fi movie?

74. Which science fiction movie sees Ethan Hawke and Jude Law switch identities?

75. Which is the only movie in the original *Planet of the Apes* series (1968-1973) not to feature the acting talents of Roddy McDowall?

76. In which 2001 science fiction movie does Seann William Scott play a trainee fire-fighter who helps save the world from

aliens?

77. Bruce Willis and Brad Pitt both starred in which 1995 science fiction movie?

78. In which 1998 science fiction blockbuster do Harry Stamper and his team of oil-rig workers save the Earth from an impending asteroid collision?

79. In which 2005 movie does actress Zooey Deschanel travel the universe in a spaceship called The Heart of Gold?

80. In what year did the BBC science fiction series *Doctor Who* first air?

81. In what year did the BBC comedy series *Red Dwarf* first air?

82. Which science fiction TV show claimed to control the horizontal and the vertical?

83. In what movie do Meredith Vickers, Charlie Holloway, Elizabeth Shaw, and a robot named David visit the planet LV-223?

84. In what year was the Academy Award winning movie *Inception* released?

85. What links the movies *Minority Report*, *Total Recall*, and *The Adjustment Bureau*?

86. What links the movies *The Fifth Element*, *Looper*, and *Surrogates*?

87. What links the movies *Resident Evil*, *The Fifth Element*, and *The Fourth Kind*?

88. In which episode of *Star Trek: The Next Generation* did Lt. Natasha Yar die?

89. In which British TV show do Abby Maitland and Connor Temple hunt creatures from Earth's past and future?

90. Which sci-fi TV show featured a dog named K-9?

91. What links *Lost in Space*, *Babylon 5*, and the *Star Trek: Deep Space 9* episode "The Siege of AR-558"?

92. What links the movies *V for Vendetta*, *The Matrix*, and *Captain America: The First Avenger*?

93. In what movie is Slim Whitman's "Indian Love Call" found to be fatal to an invading army of aliens, causing their heads to explode?

94. What British sci-fi show starred comedians Nick Frost, Kevin Eldon, and Miranda Hart?

95. Which 1970's sci-fi show was set on Moon Base Alpha?

Multiple Choice

96. Who wrote, produced and directed the 1974 film *Dark Star*?
a) Ron Howard
b) John Carpenter
c) Peter Jackson

97. Which of the following sci-fi films was directed by *Happy Days* star Ron Howard?
a) Close Encounters of the Third Kind

b) Cat-Women of the Moon
c) Cocoon

98. Who directed the 2006 science fiction film *The Island*, which sees two clones escape to track down their 'sponsors'?
a) JJ Abrams
b) James Cameron
c) Michael Bay

99. Which of the following science fiction movies won an Oscar in 1969 for "special visual effects"?
a) Dinosaurus!
b) 2001: A Space Odyssey
c) Quatermass and the Pit

100. Who wrote and directed the 2001 film *Ghosts of Mars*?
a) John Carpenter
b) Joss Whedon
c) Peter Jackson

101. Which one of the following films was not directed by Oscar winner James Cameron?
a) Predators
b) Aliens
c) The Terminator

102. Who directed the 1994 movie *Star Trek: Generations*?
a) William Shatner
b) David Carson
c) Jonathan Frakes

103. In which year was the classic science fiction movie *Forbidden Planet* first screened?
a) 1954
b) 1956
c) 1958

104. Which year saw the release of sci-fi sequels *Predator 2, RoboCop 2, Gremlins 2: The New Batch* and *Back to the Future Part III*?
a) 1986
b) 1988
c) 1990

105. The classic science fiction film *Alien* only won one Oscar, what was it for?
a) Best Actress
b) Best Film
c) Best Visual Effects

106. In which 1985 science fiction movie do a bunch of kids build their own spaceship, named the Thunder Rose?
a) Explorers
b) My Science Project
c) Real Genius

107. Which 1995 science fiction movie was based on the Philip K. Dick short story *Second Variety*?
a) Virtuosity
b) Johnny Mnemonic
c) Screamers

108. Which TV show is listed in the Guinness Book of Records as the longest running science fiction series of all time?
a) Doctor Who
b) The X Files
c) Stargate SG-1

109. In which episode of *Star Trek: The Next Generation* did physicist Steven Hawking make a guest appearance?
a) Descent
b) Data's Day
c) Elementary, Dear Data

110. Who shrunk the kids in the 1989 film *Honey, I Shrunk the Kids*?
a) Matthew Broderick
b) Rick Moranis
c) Jeff Goldblum

111. Ewan McGregor and Scarlett Johansson starred in which 2005 science fiction movie?
a) A Sound of Thunder
b) Star Wars: Episode III – Revenge of the Sith
c) The Island

112. In the 1998 movie *Deep Impact*, who discovers an asteroid on a collision course with the Earth?
a) Jeff Goldblum
b) Michael J. Fox
c) Elijah Wood

113. Who narrated the 2005 movie adaptation of Douglas Adams' *The Hitchhiker's Guide to the Galaxy*?
a) David Tennant
b) Robert Llewellyn
c) Steven Fry

114. In which 1982 movie did William Shatner appear as moon base commander Buck Murdock?
a) Megaforce
b) Parasite
c) Airplane 2: The Sequel

115. Actress Jane Fonda played the title role in which of the following movies?
a) Wonder Woman
b) Barbarella
c) Catwoman

116. In the 2010 science fiction movie *Monsters*, an alien infestation wreaks havoc in which country?
a) Australia
b) Mexico
c) Vietnam

117. Which 2010 alien invasion movie was produced and directed by brothers Greg and Colin Strause?
a) Skyline
b) Predators
c) Tron: Legacy

118. In what year did *Stargate SG-1* first air?
a) 1995
b) 1997
c) 1999

Answers – TV and Movies

1. 1955
2. The Thing
3. The Terminator
4. Minority Report
5. AVP: Alien vs. Predator
6. Star Trek (2009)
7. Mars Attacks
8. Virtuosity
9. Highlander
10. 1995
11. 1999
12. 1979
13. 1982
14. 2009
15. 1994
16. 1982
17. 1982
18. 1996
19. 1956
20. 1951
21. 1958
22. 1972
23. Danny Boyle
24. Ridley Scott
25. David Lynch
26. Tim Burton
27. Tim Burton
28. Michael Bay
29. Ridley Scott
30. Roland Emmerich
31. Steven Spielberg
32. George Pal
33. Simon Wells
34. Steven Spielberg

35. J.J Abrams
36. James Cameron
37. Fritz Lang
38. Leonard Nimoy
39. Leonard Nimoy
40. William Shatner
41. Nicholas Meyer
42. Jonathan Frakes
43. Roland Emmerich
44. Michael Bay
45. Firefly
46. Andromeda
47. Battlestar Galactica
48. Farscape
49. Sliders
50. Buck Rodgers in the 25th Century
51. Dollhouse
52. Captain Scarlet and the Mysterons
53. William Shatner
54. Flight of the Navigator
55. 28 Days Later
56. Minority Report
57. The Empire Strikes Back
58. Dead people
59. Babylon 5
60. 1993
61. 1987
62. 1993
63. 1995
64. 1966
65. Q-Less
66. City on the Edge of Forever
67. 1993
68. Morons from Outer Space
69. Brad Wright and Jonathan Glassner
70. 1962
71. Independence Day

72. Morgan Freeman
73. Starship Troopers
74. Gattaca
75. Beneath the Planet of the Apes
76. Evolution
77. 12 Monkeys
78. Armageddon
79. The Hitchhiker's Guide to the Galaxy
80. 1963
81. 1988
82. The Outer Limits
83. Prometheus
84. 2010
85. They are all based on short stories by Philip K Dick
86. actor Bruce Willis
87. actress Milla Jovovich
88. Skin of Evil
89. Primeval
90. Doctor Who
91. actor Bill Mummy
92. actor Hugo Weaving
93. Mars Attacks
94. Hyperdrive
95. Space 1999
96. b) John Carpenter
97. c) Cocoon
98. c) Michael Bay
99. b) 2001: A Space Odyssey
100. a) John Carpenter
101. a) Predators
102. b) David Carson
103. b) 1956
104. c) 1990
105. c) Best Visual Effects
106. a) Explorers
107. c) Screamers
108. a) Doctor Who

109. a) Descent
110. b) Rick Moranis
111. c) The Island
112. c) Elijah Wood
113. c) Steven Fry
114. c) Airplane 2: The Sequel
115. b) Barbarella
116 b) Mexico
117. a) Skyline
118. b) 1997

Characters and Actors

1. Who starred as Sam Beckett in the classic TV show *Quantum Leap*?

2. Which actor played Steve Austin in the classic sci-fi show *The Six Million Dollar Man*?

3. Which actress starred as Sarah Connor in the TV series *Terminator: The Sarah Connor Chronicles*?

4. Actor Hayden Christensen is famous for playing which *Star Wars* character?

5. Who played Lando Calrissian in the original *Star Wars* movies?

6. Which actress played Padame Amidala in the *Star Wars* prequel films?

7. Who played Jedi Master Mace Windu in the *Star Wars* prequel films?

8. Who provided the voice of Darth Vader for the original *Star Wars* films?

9. Who played Obi-Wan Kenobi in the original *Star Wars* films?

10. Who played Princess Leia Organa in the original *Star*

Wars films?

11. Harrison Ford played which character in the original *Star Wars* films?

12. Who played the young Anakin Skywalker in *Star Wars: The Phantom Menace*?

13. In *Return of the Jedi*, who commands the former cruise ship Home One during the Battle of Endor?

14. Who killed Darth Vader's mother?

15. In *Star Wars Episode IV: A New Hope*, who calls Chewbacca a "walking carpet"?

16. In *Return of the Jedi*, which character famously said "our cruisers can't repel fire-power of that magnitude"?

17. In *Stargate SG*-1, Samantha Carter is a doctor of what?

18. Who played Samantha Carter in *Stargate SG-1*?

19. Who was the Chief Medical Officer of Stargate Command through seasons 1-9 of *Stargate SG-1*?

20. Who played Teal'c in *Stargate SG-1*?

21. Who played Dr. Daniel Jackson in *Stargate SG-1*?

22. Who played Jack O'Neill in *Stargate SG-1*?

23. Who played Chief Master Sergeant Walter Harriman in *Stargate SG-1*?

24. In *Stargate Atlantis*, what is Dr. McKay's first name?

25. In *Stargate SG-1*, what is the name of Teal'c's son?

26. In *Stargate SG-1*, what was the name of Jack O'Neill's dead son?

27. Who played Vala Mal Doran in *Stargate SG-1*?

28. Who played Lt. Colonel Cameron Mitchell in *Stargate SG-1*?

29. Which actor plays the *Stargate* character Dr. Meredith Rodney McKay?

30. Which actor plays Dr. Nicholas Rush in *Stargate Universe*?

31. In the *Babylon 5* episode "The Fall of Night", who reveals himself for the first time in the Babylon 5's zen garden?

32. In the fifth season of *Babylon 5*, which captain takes command of Babylon 5 following Captain Sheridan's resignation from Earth Force?

33. Mariel, Daggair and Timov are the wives of which alien diplomat?

34. Which *Babylon 5* character was played by actress Mira Furlan?

35. Which *Babylon 5* character was played by actor Bruce Boxleitner?

36. Which *Babylon 5* character was played by actor Jerry Doyle?

37. Which *Babylon 5* character was played by actor Peter Jurasik?

38. Which *Babylon 5* character was played by actor Andreas Katsulas?

39. Which *Babylon 5* actor also appeared as a T-bird in the 1978 movie *Grease*?

40. *Babylon 5* actors Bruce Boxleitner and Peter Jurasik both appeared as anthropomorphic computer programs in which 1982 science fiction movie?

41. According to the 2009 movie *Star Trek*, what is Uhura's first name?

42. In *Star Trek*, what is Dr McCoy's first name?

43. What was the name of Spock's father?

44. In *Star Trek: The Next Generation*, what colour are Lieutenant Commander Data's eyes?

45. In *Star Trek: The Next Generation*, what was the name of Worf's father?

46. In *Star Trek: The Next Generation*, Alexander Rozhenko was the son of which Enterprise crew member?

47. In *Star Trek: The Next Generation*, what was the name of Worf's foster father?

48. In the *Star Trek: Deep Space Nine* episode "The Nagus", what is the name of Grand Nagus Zek's son?

49. In *Star Trek: Deep Space Nine*, what is Benjamin Sisko's middle name?

50. In *Star Trek: Deep Space Nine*, what is the name of

Quark's mother, also known as Moogie?

51. In *Star Trek: Deep Space Nine*, what was the name of Quark's father?

52. In *Star Trek: Deep Space Nine*, what is the Cardassian tailor Garak's first name?

53. In *Star Trek: Deep Space Nine*, what is the name of Garak's father?

54. In the movie *Star Trek: Nemesis*, who stages a successful coup to become Praetor of the Romulan Empire?

55. Who killed Duras, son of Toral?

56. Who killed Duras, son of Ja'rod?

57. Lursa and B'Etor were the sisters of which prominent Klingon aristocrat?

58. Who was the first child to be born aboard the USS Voyager?

59. Captain Kathryn Janeway was born and raised in which U.S state?

60. Who played Dr. Tolian Soran in the movie *Star Trek: Generations*?

61. Which *Star Trek* character has been portrayed by actors Mark Lenard, Jonathan Simpson, and Ben Cross?

62. The *Star Trek* characters Brunt, Weyoun and Commander Shran were all played by which actor?

63. Which actor reprised the role of Scotty in the 2009 movie

remake of *Star Trek*?

64. Which actor played the role of Benjamin Sisko in *Star Trek: Deep Space Nine*?

65. Which actor played the role of Chief Miles O'Brien in *Star Trek: The Next Generation* and *Star Trek: Deep Space Nine*?

66. Which actor played the role of Kira Nerys in *Star Trek: Deep Space Nine*?

67. Which actor played the role of Jadzia Dax in *Star Trek: Deep Space Nine*?

68. Which actor played the role of Quark in *Star Trek: Deep Space Nine*?

69. Which actor played the role of Grand Nagus Zek in *Star Trek: Deep Space Nine*?

70. Which actor played the role of Odo in *Star Trek: Deep Space Nine*?

71. Which actor played the role of William Riker in *Star Trek: The Next Generation*?

72. Which actor played the role of Worf in *Star Trek: The Next Generation* and *Star Trek: Deep Space Nine*?

73. Which actor played the role of Geordie LaForge in *Star Trek: The Next Generation*?

74. Which actor played the role of Lieutenant Commander Data in *Star Trek: The Next Generation*?

75. Which actor played the role of Dianna Troi in *Star Trek: The Next Generation*?

76. Which actor played the role of Gowron in *Star Trek: The Next Generation* and *Star Trek: Deep Space Nine*?

77. Which actor played the role of Commander Trip Tucker in *Star Trek: Enterprise*?

78. Which actor played the role of Malcolm Reed in *Star Trek: Enterprise*?

79. Who played the Vulcan officer T'Pol in *Star Trek: Enterprise*?

80. Which actor played the role of Captain Kathryn Janeway in *Star Trek: Voyager*?

81. Which actor played the role of Tuvok in *Star Trek: Voyager*?

82. Which actor played the role of Tom Paris in *Star Trek: Voyager*?

83. Which actor played the role of The Doctor in *Star Trek: Voyager*?

84. Which actor played the psychopath Lon Suder in *Star Trek: Voyager*?

85. Which actor played the role of Seven of Nine in *Star Trek: Voyager*?

86. Which actor played the role of Chakotay in *Star Trek: Voyager*?

87. Which actor plays Captain Jonathan Archer in *Star Trek: Enterprise*?

88. In *Star Trek: The Next Generation*, which actor plays the role of Dr. Noonien Sung?

89. Which star of the original *Star Trek* series died of pneumonia in July 2004 after battling Parkinson's disease, diabetes, interstitial lung disease and Alzheimer's?

90. Which *Star Trek: The Next Generation* character was played by Michelle Forbes?

91. In *Star Trek, The Next Generation*, Captain Morgan Bateson, played by Kelsey Grammer, was captain of which Starfleet vessel?

92. In *Star Trek: The Next Generation*, who built the androids Data, Lore and B4?

93. In *Star Trek: Voyager*, who created the Emergency Medical Holographic program (E.M.H)?

94. In *Star Trek: Voyager*, what is the name of holodeck character Captain Proton's arch enemy?

95. In which episode of *Star Trek: Voyager* did wrestler Dwayne Johnson, aka The Rock, make a guest appearance?

96. In *Star Trek: The Next Generation*, what is the name of Data's cat?

97. In the animated series *Futurama* what is Dr Zoidberg's first name?

98. In *Futurama*, what is the name of Bender's bearded twin brother?

99. In *Futurama*, what is the robot Bender's surname?

100. In *Futurama* what is the robot Bender's middle name?

101. Who starred as astronaut John Crichton in the quirky sci-fi series *Farscape*?

102. Which actress played the renegade Peacekeeper officer Aeryn Sun in the TV series *Farscape*?

103. Who played Doctor Who's favourite travelling companion, Rose Tyler, in the TV series *Doctor Who*?

104. Who played Doctor Who's companion Sarah Jane Smith in *Doctor Who* and the spin-off series *The Sarah Jane Adventures*?

105. In the TV series *Torchwood*, who plays Captain Jack Harkness?

106. Who was the first actor to play the role of The Doctor in the BBC TV show *Doctor Who*?

107. Who was the second actor to play the role of The Doctor in the BBC TV show *Doctor Who*?

108. Who was the third actor to play the role of The Doctor in the BBC TV show *Doctor Who*?

109. Who was the fourth actor to play the role of The Doctor in the BBC TV show *Doctor Who*?

110. Who was the fifth actor to play the role of The Doctor in the BBC TV show *Doctor Who*?

111. In 2005, David Tennant became the tenth Doctor in the BBC series *Doctor Who*. Who was the ninth Doctor?

112. In what year did Sylvester McCoy become the seventh

incarnation of The Doctor?

113. *Doctor Who* character Harry Sullivan travelled through time and space as a companion to which Doctor?

114. Who made his first TV appearance as The Doctor on January 1st 2010, becoming the eleventh actor to play the role?

115. In which sci-fi TV show did actor Adam Baldwin play a gun-toting outlaw and mercenary by the name of Jayne Cobb?

116. Which actress played the character Inara Serra in the TV show *Firefly*?

117. Which actress played the character River Tam in the TV show *Firefly*?

118. "I am a leaf on the wind, watch how I soar" were the final words of which *Firefly* character?

119. Who starred as Captain Malcolm Reynolds in the the sci-fi series *Firefly*?

120. Who played William Adama in the 2000's re-imagined series of *Battlestar Galactica*?

121. Edward James Olmos' son, Bodie Olmos, played which character in the 2000's re-imagined series of *Battlestar Galactica*?

122. Dirk Benedict and Katee Sackhoff are the male and female incarnations of which *Battlestar Galactica* character?

123. In the 2000's re-imagined series of *Battlestar Galactica*, what is Starbuck's real name?

124. Which *Battlestar Galactica* character was played by Terry Carter and Michael Hogan respectively?

125. In the re-imagined series of *Battlestar Galactica*, who was President of the Colonies immediately prior to Laura Roslin?

126. Richard Hatch was *Battlestar Galactica*'s original Captain Apollo, but which character did the actor play in the 2000's re-imagined series?

127. In the 2000's re-imagined series of *Battlestar Galactica*, what was the name of Romo Lampkin's cat?

128. Who played the Number Three Cylons, including the Cylon known as D'Anna, in the 2000's re-imagined series of *Battlestar Galactica*?

129. Who played the Number Six Cylons, including the Cylon known as Caprica Six, in the 2000's re-imagined series of *Battlestar Galactica*?

130. In the *Battlestar Galactica* episode "Lay Down Your Burdens Part 2", who is named President of the Colonies?

131. Who starred as Zoe Greystone in the TV series *Caprica*?

132. Who played Dave Lister in the BBC comedy series *Red Dwarf*?

133. Who played Arnold Rimmer in the BBC comedy series *Red Dwarf*?

134. In the British comedy series *Red Dwarf*, what is Arnold Rimmer's middle name?

135. In the British comedy series *Red Dwarf*, what was the

name of Lister's pet cat, the Holy Mother of the evolved cat species?

136. Red Dwarf character Dave Lister was abandoned in a cardboard box when he was a baby. What was written on the side of the box?

137. Hattie Hayridge famously portrayed the female incarnation of which senile computer?

138. American actor Mac McDonald is best known for his portrayal of which character in the British sci-fi comedy *Red Dwarf*?

139. Scottish actress and singer Clare Grogan is best known to sci-fi fans for her portrayal of which character in the British sci-fi comedy *Red Dwarf*?

140. Which 1990s TV show centred on the characters Zev, Kai and Stanley Tweedle?

141. What was the name of the robot maid in *The Jetsons*?

142. In *The Jetsons*, what was the name of the Jetsons' family dog?

143. In *Sliders*, what is the name of Quinn Mallory's cat?

144. Who starred as Captain Nathan Bridger in the TV show *seaQuest DSV*?

145. In the 2009 remake of *V*, the alien Anna was played by which actress?

146. In which TV show does Amanda Tapping star as Dr. Helen Magnus?

147. Who starred as Jamie Sommers in the 2007 remake of *The Bionic Woman*?

148. Which actress starred as Echo in Joss Whedon's short-lived sci-fi series, *Dollhouse*?

149. In the TV series *Dollhouse*, which character is played by actor Tahmoh Pennikett?

150. Which actor played professor Maximilian Arturo in the TV show *Sliders*?

151. In which 90's science fiction TV show did actress Sabrina Lloyd play inter-dimensional poetry student Wade Welles?

152. Which actor played alien physics professor Dick Solomon in the science fiction comedy series *Third Rock from the Sun*?

153. Which actor played portly police officer Don in the science fiction comedy series *Third Rock from the Sun*?

154. In which sci-fi TV show does actor Noah Wyle star as Tom Mason, a history professor turned resistance fighter?

155. In the 1968 movie *Planet of the Apes*, what name does Taylor give to his mute human girlfriend?

156. In the *Back to the Future* movies, what is Doc Brown's first name?

157. Who played Tron and Alan Bradley in the 1982 movie *Tron* and the 2010 movie *Tron: Legacy*?

158. Sheriff Jack Carter, portrayed by Colin Ferguson, is sheriff of which fictional town?

159. Who starred as helicopter pilot MacReady in John

Carpenter's *The Thing*?

160. Who stars as computer expert David Levinson in the alien invasion movie *Independence Day*?

161. In the 1996 movie Independence Day, who played United States President Thomas Whitmore?

162. Who starred as Detective John Anderton in the movie *Minority Report*?

163. Will Smith starred as which agent in the *Men in Black* movies?

164. Who starred as Tony Stark in the 2008 movie *Iron Man*?

165. Who starred as Neo in *The Matrix* movie trilogy?

166. Which actor played the role of Agent Smith in *The Matrix*?

167. What was the name of Laurence Fishburne's character in *The Matrix*?

168. Who starred as Logan 5 in the 1976 movie *Logan's Run*?

169. Which actor played the role of Dr Zaius in the 1968 movie *Planet of the Apes*?

170. Who starred as Chris Kelvin in the 2002 remake of *Solaris*?

171. Who played the mathematician Dr. Ian Malcolm in the movie *Jurassic Park*?

172. Who played the palaeontologist Dr. Alan Grant in the movie *Jurassic Park*?

173. Which celebrated British actor/director played billionaire John Hammond in the movie *Jurassic Park*?

174. What was the name of Sigourney Weaver's character in the movie *Alien*?

175. Who starred as Riddick in the movies *Pitch Black* and *The Chronicles of Riddick*?

176. Who starred as Terl in the 2000 film adaptation of L. Ron Hubbard's *Battlefield Earth*?

177. Who starred as Colonel Jack O'Neil in the 1994 film *Stargate*?

178. Who stared as Cleric John Preston in the 2002 movie *Equilibrium*?

179. Actress Hannah Spearitt achieved fame with which pop group before joining the cast of *Primeval*?

180. Which actor reprised the role of James T. Kirk in the 2009 movie remake of *Star Trek*?

181. Which actor reprised the role of Dr. Leonard McCoy in the 2009 movie remake of *Star Trek*?

182. In the British comedy series *Red Dwarf*, what is the robot Kryten's middle name?

183. What was the name of the astronaut toy in the *Toy Story* movies?

184. In *Star Trek: Deep Space Nine*, what was Kai Winn's given name?

185. "Racetrack", "Flat Top", "Crashdown", "Chuckles" and "Skulls" are all names of what?

186. By what callsign was *Battlestar Galactica* officer Karl Agathon known?

187. By what callsign was *Battlestar Galactica* Viper pilot Brendon Costanza known?

188. By what callsign was *Battlestar Galactica*'s commander William Adama known in his younger days as a Viper pilot?

189. In which U.S state was James T. Kirk raised?

190. In what movie does former *Crystal Maze* presenter Richard O'Brien appear as the alien Mr. Hand?

191. In the TV show Buck Rodgers in the 25th Century, which character was played by actress/model Erin Gray ?

192. In *Star Trek: Deep Space Nine*, the full name given to Odo by the Cardassians is Odo'ital. What does it mean?

193. Who played the talking ape Caesar in the 1972 film *Conquest of the Planet of the Apes*?

Multiple Choice

194. In *Babylon 5*, Commander Jeffrey Sinclair was born on which world?
a) Proxima 3
b) Mars
c) Minbar

195. In which city was *Stargate*'s Colonel Jack O'Neill born?
a) Minneapolis
b) Indianapolis
c) Chicago

196. Which *Stargate SG-1* character was played by Bill Dow, and went on to make guest appearances in both *Stargate Atlantis* and *Stargate Universe*?
a) Sergeant Siler
b) Dr. Lee
c) Chief Master Sergeant Walter Harriman

197. In *Stargate SG*-1, which character is referred to as "The destroyer of worlds"?
a) Osiris
b) Lineya
c) Bra'tac

198. Which *Stargate SG-1* character gives birth to the evil child Adria, also known as the Orici?
a) Samantha Carter
b) Janet Fraiser
c) Vala Mal Doran

199. Which character died at the end of the *Stargate SG-1* episode "Heroes, Part 2"?
a) General Hammond
b) Dr. Jackson
c) Dr. Fraiser

200. In *Stargate SG-1*, what is the name of Teal'c's wife?
a) Drey'auc
b) Teyla
c) Sha're

201. In *Stargate SG-1*, who killed Teal'c's father?
a) Cronus

b) Bra'tac
c) Apophis

202. Which actor plays the role of Ronon Dex in *Stargate Atlantis*?
a) Lani Tupu
b) Jason Momoa
c) Christopher Judge

203. Which alien is a major player in Babylon 5's criminal underworld?
a) Nagrath
b) Na'Toth
c) Draal

204. In the *Babylon 5* episode "Soul Mates", which of his three wives did Londo Mollari choose not to divorce?
a) Mariel
b) Timov
c) Daggair

205. In *Babylon 5*, who was the first human to fight in the Mutai?
a) Walker Smith
b) John Sheridan
c) Michael Garibaldi

206. Which of these *Babylon 5* actors did NOT appear in the 1982 movie *Tron*?
a) Bruce Boxleitner
b) Peter Jurasik
c) Jerry Doyle

207. Actor and comedian Peter Mayhew was the man inside the costume of which *Star Wars* character?
a) Chewbacca
b) C-3P0

c) R2-D2

208. Which of the following is NOT a real Lord of the Sith in the expanded *Star Wars* universe?
a) Darth Zhorrid
b) Darth Uglacon
c) Darth Scabrous

209. Which of the following is NOT a real Lord of the Sith in the expanded *Star Wars* universe?
a) Darth Tyranus
b) Darth Venemis
c) Darth Sploder

210. How did Han Solo acquire the Millennium Falcon?
a) He stole it
b) He won it in a bet
c) It was a gift

211. During which episode of *Star Trek: The Next Generation* is the character Chief O'Brien first seen?
a) The Icarus Factor
b) Encounter at Farpoint
c) Lonely Among Us

212. Which *Star Trek: Deep Space Nine* character also made an appearance in the first episode of *Star Trek: Voyager*?
a) Quark
b) Odo
c) Captain Sisko

213. In *Star Trek: Deep Space Nine*, Ziyal was the daughter of which Cardassian officer?
a) Gul Dukat
b) Gul Evek
c) Legate Damar

214. Eric Bana played which Romulan bad-guy in the 2009 movie *Star Trek*?
a) Nero
b) Shinzon
c) Valdore

215. Which actress played Spock's mother, Amanda Grayson, in the 2009 film *Star Trek*?
a) Lena Headey
b) Winona Ryder
c) Majel Barrett

216. In *Star Trek III: The Search for Spock*, which actor played the Klingon commander Kruge?
a) Christopher Plummer
b) Michael Dorn
c) Christopher Lloyd

217. Which actress played Lt. Valeris in *Star Trek VI: The Undiscovered Country*?
a) Kim Cattral
b) Kirstie Alley
c) Terry Farrell

218. In the *Voyager* episode "The Voyager Conspiracy", which alien scientist constructs an experimental graviton catapult?
a) Forra Gegan
b) Tash
c) Exeter

219. In the *Deep Space Nine* episode "The House of Quark", Quark marries which Klingon female?
a) Grilka
b) Lursa
c) K'Ehleyr

220. In *Star Trek: Deep Space Nine*, which one of Dax's

previous hosts was a psychopathic killer?
a) Torias
b) Curzon
c) Joran

221. In *Star Trek: The Next Generation*, what is the name of chief O'Brien's eldest child?
a) Shaun
b) Molly
c) Kirayoshi

222. In which of the following Star Trek films does Spock's mother, Amanda Grayson, NOT appear?
a) Star Trek III: The Search For Spock
b) Star Trek IV: The Voyage Home
c) Star Trek V: The Final Frontier

223. In the *Voyager* episode "The Q and the Grey", who becomes the mother of Q's child?
a) Kes
b) Captain Janeway
c) Q

224. Which actor has appeared in more episodes of *Doctor Who* than any other?
a) William Hartnell
b) Jon Pertwee
c) Tom Baker

225. Which *Battlestar Galactica* character was played by actor James Callis?
a) Tom Zarek
b) Romo Lampkin
c) Gaius Baltar

226. Echo, Victor, Sierra, and Adelle DeWitt are all characters in which science fiction TV show?

a) Dollhouse
b) Blake's 7
c) Captain Scarlet and the Mysterons

227. In what BBC Sitcom did Nicholas Lyndhurst play a time travelling polygamist?
a) Goodnight Sweetheart
b) Red Dwarf
c) Hyperdrive

228. Who starred as Ira Kane in the 2001 tongue-in-cheek science fiction movie *Evolution*?
a) David Duchovny
b) Orlando Jones
c) Dan Aykroyd

229. Which actress starred as Irene Cassini in the 1997 movie *Gattaca*?
a) Julia Roberts
b) Uma Thurman
c) Julie Benz

230. Which *Star Trek: The Next Generation* actor appeared in the 1996 blockbuster *Independence Day* as scientist Dr. Brackish Okun?
a) Brent Spiner
b) Armin Shimerman
c) Leonard Nimoy

231. Who starred in the 1960 film adaptation of H.G Wells' *The Time Machine*?
a) Guy Pearce
b) Rod Taylor
c) James Mason

232. What was the name of the talking dolphin in *SeaQuest DSV*?

a) Fermi
b) Copernicus
c) Darwin

233. Who starred in the title role of the 2005 sci-fi action film *Aeon Flux*?
a) Milla Jovovich
b) Natasha Henstridge
c) Charlize Theron

234. Which actor played an animatronic gunslinger in the 1973 film *Westworld*?
a) Charlton Heston
b) Yul Brynner
c) Lorne Greene

235. Who provided the voice of Marvin the robot in the 2005 film adaptation of *The Hitchhiker's Guide to the Galaxy*?
a) Alan Rickman
b) Chris Langham
c) Charlie Brooker

236. Which actress played the role of Trillian in the 2005 film adaptation of *The Hitchhiker's Guide to the Galaxy*?
a) Alessandra Torresani
b) Eliza Dushku
c) Zooey Deschanel

237. In the TV series *Primeval*, what is the name of Abby's pet dinosaur?
a) Spike
b) Rex
c) Connor

238. Which *Star Trek: Enterprise* actor also made regular appearances in *Stargate Atlantis* as the Wraith hybrid Michael?

a) Scott Bakula
b) Dominic Keating
c) Connor Trinneer

239. Who starred as Lt. Christopher Blair in the 1999 film adaptation of the computer game *Wing Commander*?
a) Freddie Prinze Jr.
b) Skeet Ulrich
c) Morgan Weisser

240. In which episode of *Doctor Who* did The Doctor first meet River Song?
a) The Time of Angels
b) Silence in the Library
c) The Doctor's Daughter

241. According to *The Hitchhiker's Guide to the Galaxy* who designed the Norwegian fjords?
a) Slartibartfast
b) Flippertybumwak
c) Progon Jaynus

242. Alex Rogan was the last what?
a) Man on Earth
b) Space-Mohican
c) Starfighter

Answers – Characters and Actors

1. Scott Bakula
2. Lee Majors
3. Lena Headley
4. Anakin Skywalker
5. Billy Dee Williams
6. Natalie Portman
7. Samuel L. Jackson
8. James Earl Jones
9. Alec Guinnes
10. Carrie Fisher
11. Han Solo
12. Jake Lloyd
13. Admiral Ackbar
14. The Sand People (Tuskan Raiders)
15. Princess Leia Organa
16. Admiral Ackbar
17. Astrophysics
18. Amanda Tapping
19. Dr. Janet Fraiser
20. Christopher Judge
21. Michael Shanks
22. Richard Dean Anderson
23. Gary Jones
24. Meredith
25. Rya'c
26. Charlie
27. Claudia Black
28. Ben Browder
29. David Hewlett
30. Robert Carlyle
31. Ambassador Kosh
32. Captain Lockley
33. Londo Molari
34. Delenn

35. John Sheridan
36. Michael Garibaldi
37. Londo Molari
38. G'Kar
39. Jeff Conaway
40. Tron
41. Nyota
42. Leonard
43. Sarek
44. Yellow
45. Mogh
46. Worf
47. Sergei Rozhenko
48. Krax
49. Lafayette
50. Ishka
51. Keldar
52. Elim
53. Enabran Tain
54. Shinzon of Remus
55. Jonathan Archer (and the crew of the USS Enterprise)
56. Worf, son of Mogh
57. Duras
58. Naomi Wildman
59. Indiana
60. Malcolm McDowell
61. Sarek
62. Jeffrey Combs
63. Simon Peg
64. Avery Brookes
65. Colm Meaney
66. Nana Visitor
67. Terry Farrell
68. Armin Shimerman
69. Wallace Shawn
70. Rene Auberjonois
71. Jonathan Frakes

72. Michael Dorn
73. LeVar Burton
74. Brent Spiner
75. Marina Sirtis
76. Robert O'Reilly
77. Connor Trinneer
78. Dominic Keating
79. Jolene Blalock
80. Kate Mulgrew
81. Tim Russ
82. Robert Duncan McNeill
83. Robert Picardo
84. Brad Dourif
85. Jeri Ryan
86. Robert Beltran
87. Scott Bakula
88. Brent Spiner
89. James Doohan
90. Ro Larren
91. USS Bozeman
92. Dr Noonian Soong
93. Dr. Lewis Zimmerman
94. Dr. Chaotica
95. Tsunkatse
96. Spot
97. John
98. Flexo
99. Rodriguez
100. Bending
101. Ben Browder
102. Claudia Black
103. Billie Piper
104. Elisabeth Sladen
105. John Barrowman
106. William Hartnell
107. Patrick Troughton
108. John Pertwee

109. Tom Baker
110. Peter Davison
111. Christopher Eccleston
112. 1987
113. Tom Baker (Fourth Doctor)
114. Matt Smith
115. Firefly
116. Morena Baccarin
117. Summer Glau
118. Hoban Washburne (Wash)
119. Nathan Fillion
120. Edward James Olmos
121. Hot Dog
122. Starbuck
123. Kara Thrace
124. Colonel Tigh
125. Richard Adar
126. Tom Zarek
127. Lance
128. Lucy Lawless
129. Tricia Helfer
130. Gaius Baltar
131. Alessandra Torresani
132. Craig Charles
133. Chris Barrie
134. Judas
135. Frankenstein
136. Ouroboros
137. Holly
138. Captain Hollister
139. Kristine Kochanski
140. Lexx
141. Rosie
142. Astro
143. Schrödinger
144. Roy Scheider
145. Morena Baccarin

146. Sanctuary
147. Michelle Ryan
148. Eliza Dushku
149. Paul Ballard
150. John Rhys-Davies
151. Sliders
152. John Lithgow
153. Wayne Knight
154. Falling Skies
155. Nova
156. Emmett
157. Bruce Boxleitner
158. Eureka
159. Kurt Russel
160. Jeff Goldblum
161. Bill Pullman
162. Tom Cruise
163. Agent J
164. Robert Downey Jr
165. Keanu Reeves
166. Hugo Weaving
167. Morpheus
168. Michael York
169. Maurice Evans
170. George Clooney
171. Jeff Goldblum
172. Sam Neil
173. Richard Attenborough
174. Ellen Ripley
175. Vin Diesel
176. John Travolta
177. Kurt Russel
178. Christian Bale
179. S Club 7
180. Chris Pine
181. Karl Urban
182. 2X4B

183. Buzz Lightyear
184. Adami
185. Pilots in Battlestar Galactica
186. Helo
187. Hot Dog
188. Husker
189. Iowa
190. Dark City
191. Wilma Deering
192. Unknown sample
193. Roddy McDowall
194. b) Mars
195. c) Chicago
196. b) Dr. Lee
197. b) Lineya
198. c) Vala Mal Doran
199. c) Dr. Fraiser
200. a) Drey'auc
201. a) Cronus
202. b) Jason Momoa
203. a) Nagrath
204. b) Timov
205. a) Walker Smith
206. c) Jerry Doyle
207. a) Chewbacca
208. b) Darth Uglacon
209. c) Darth Sploder
210. b) He won it in a bet
211. b) Encounter at Farpoint
212. a) Quark
213. a) Gul Dukat
214. a) Nero
215. b) Winona Ryder
216. c) Christopher Lloyd
217. b) Kim Cattral
218. b) Tash
219. a) Grilka

220. c) Joran
221. b) Molly
222. a) Star Trek III: The Search For Spock
223. c) Q
224. c) Tom Baker
225. c) Gaius Baltar
226. a) Dollhouse
227. a) Goodnight Sweetheart
228. a) David Duchovny
229. b) Uma Thurman
230. a) Brent Spiner
231. b) Rod Taylor
232. c) Darwin
233. c) Charlize Theron
234. b) Yul Brynner
235. a) Alan Rickman
236. c) Zooey Deschanel
237. b) Rex
238. c) Connor Trinneer
239. a) Freddie Prinze Jr
240. b) Silence in the Library
241. a) Slartibartfast
242. c) Starfighter

Miscellaneous

1. If 42 is the ultimate answer to life, the universe and everything, what is the ultimate question?

2. According to Mon Mothma in *Return of the Jedi*, how many Bothans died to bring information about the Second Death Star to the Rebel Alliance?

3. In which city is the *Doctor Who* spin-off series *Torchwood* set?

4. How many pips does a Federation Starfleet Captain wear on his/her collar?

5. Dr. Gordon Freeman is the main protagonist in which series of science fiction computer games?

6. In the *Star Trek* universe, what does the acronym U.F.P stand for?

7. In the *Stargate SG-1* episode "The Quest", who's memories are downloaded into Daniel Jackson's mind?

8. What was the title of the official comic book prequel to the 2009 movie *Star Trek*?

9. In what year did *Star Trek* creator Gene Roddenberry die?

10. For what organization did Captain Scarlet work?

11. In the movie *Blade Runner*, what animal does Tyrell have in his office?

12. In *Battlestar Galactica* what is the Galactica and its rag-tag fleet looking for?

13. The short-lived sci-fi series *Dark Angel* was set in which city?

14. The pop group Duran Duran took their name from which classic science fiction movie?

15. In *Star Trek: The Next Generation*, what species of fish does Captain Picard have in his ready room?

16. In *Firefly*, what name does Jayne give to his favourite gun?

17. In the original *Battlestar Galactica*, what was the name of Boxey's robotic daggit?

18. At the end of *Star Wars: The Empire Strikes Back*, Han Solo is frozen and encased in what substance?

19. How many crew members were aboard the USCSS Nostromo at the beginning of the movie *Alien*?

20. In the *Hitchhiker's Guide to the Galaxy*, who is described as "the triple-breasted whore of Eroticon Six"?

21. According to *The Hitchhiker's Guide to the Galaxy*, what is the best drink in existence?

22. Complete this famous Yoda quote. "Do or do not. There is no..."

23. Complete this famous Yoda quote. "Luminous beings are we, not this..."

24. Complete this Yoda quote from *Star Wars – Episode III: Revenge of the Sith.* "Rejoice for those around you who transform into the Force. Mourn them do not. Miss them do not. Attachment leads to jealousy..."

25. Complete the following Darth Vader quote. "The Force is strong with you, young Skywalker, but you are..."

26. Complete the following Darth Vader quote. "Search your feelings, you..."

27. In which episode of *Red Dwarf* would you hear the words "nureek", "rutut", "hununga" and "squilookle"?

28. In what movie did Sigourney Weaver famously shout "Get away from her, you bitch!"

29. In the *Red Dwarf* episode "Legion", why is Kryten reluctant to go to red alert?

30. Complete the following Gowron quote from *Star Trek: Deep Space Nine.* "Come with me, Worf; glory awaits you..."

31. Complete the following quote from *2001: A Space Odyssey.* "I'm sorry, Dave, I'm..."

32. Complete the following *Flash Gordon* quote. "Flash, I love you, but we only have..."

33. In which 1999 science fiction movie would you hear the line "There is no spoon"?

34. Complete this famous Spock quote from *Star Trek: The Wrath of Khan.* "I have been, and always shall be..."

35. Complete this famous Spock quote from *Star Trek: The Wrath of Khan*. "The needs of the many..."

36. Complete the following famous movie quote. "You maniacs! You blew it up! Damn you!..."

37. Complete the following famous movie quote. "Take your stinking paws of me, you..."

38. Complete the following famous movie quote. "Help me Obi-wan Kenobi. You're my..."

39. Complete the following famous movie quote. "Gort! Klaatu barada..."

40. In which classic sci-fi movie would you hear the phrase "Klaatu barada nikto"?

Multiple Choice

41. Complete the following Arthur Dent quote from *The Hitchhiker's Guide to the Galaxy*. "I never could get the hang of..."
a) ...trousers
b) ...hangovers
c) ...Thursdays

42. In *Star Trek: The Next Generation*, the Battle of Wolf 359 took place in what future year?
a) 2367
b) 2375
c) 2383

43. In the movie *Star Trek: First Contact*, the Enterprise travels back in time to what year?
a) 2023
b) 2043
c) 2063

44. Which "space trading" computer game was developed by David Braben and Ian Bell and was originally published by Acornsoft in 1984?
a) Elite
b) Freelancer
c) Escape Velocity

45. In what year was the massively multi-player online game *EVE Online* first released?
a) 2003
b) 2004
c) 2005

46. In what year was the massively multi-player online game *Star Trek Online* launched?
a) 2006
b) 2008
c) 2010

47. According to the animated series *Futurama* who was the first Emperor of the Moon?
a) William Shatner
b) John Stuart
c) Al Gore

48. In the 1968 movie *Barbarella*, how do people from Earth make love?
a) In zero gravity
b) By swallowing a pill
c) In groups of five or more

Answers – Miscellaneous

1. What do you get if you multiply six by nine?
2. Many
3. Cardiff
4. 4
5. Half Life
6. United Federation of Planets
7. Merlin
8. Star Trek: Countdown
9. 1991
10. Spectrum
11. Owl
12. Earth
13. Seattle
14. Barbarella
15. Lion Fish
16. Vera
17. Muffit
18. Carbonite
19. 8
20. Eccentrica Galumbits
21. Pan Galactic Gargle Blaster
22. ...try
23. ...crude matter
24. ...the shadow of greed, that is
25. ...not a Jedi yet
26. ...know it to be true
27. Duct Soup
28. Aliens
29. It means changing the bulb
30. ...on Cardassia
31. ...afraid I can't do that
32. ...fourteen hours to save the Earth
33. The Matrix
34. ...your friend

35. ...out weigh the needs of the few
36. ...Damn you all to hell
37. ...damn dirty ape
38. ...only hope
39. ...nikto
40. The Day the Earth Stood Still
41. c) ...Thursdays
42. a) 2367
43. c) 2063
44. a) Elite
45. a) 2003
46. c) 2010
47. c) Al Gore
48. b) By swallowing a pill

Printed in Great Britain
by Amazon.co.uk, Ltd.,
Marston Gate.